BEVERLY LEWIS

Illustrations by
CHERI BLADHOLM

JUST LIKE MAMA

BETHANY
BACKYARD®
www.bethanyhouse.com

JUST LIKE MAMA

Text copyright © 2002 by Beverly Lewis.
Illustrations copyright © 2002 by Cheri Bladholm.

Design: Lookout Design Group, Inc.
Printed in China.

Library of Congress Cataloging-in-Publication Data

Lewis, Beverly, 1949-
Just Like Mama / by Beverly Lewis ; illustrated by Cheri Bladholm.
p. cm.
Summary: Susie Mae wants to be just like her mama, so she follows her around
all day trying to do all the chores Mama does on their Amish farm.

ISBN 0-7642-2507-3 (alk. paper)

[1. Mothers and daughters—Fiction. 2. Farm life—Fiction. 3. Amish—Fiction.]
I. Bladholm, Cheri, ill. II. Title.
PZ7.L58464 Ju 2002
[E]—dc21
2002006132

"...for the Lord seeth not as man seeth; for man looketh
on the outward appearance, but the Lord looketh on the heart."

— I SAMUEL 16:7 KJV

For Catherine Smithers, her mama, and grandmama,
with delightful memories of Ohio visits.
—B.L.

To the Meck and Landis families
for your inspiration, prayers, warmth, and humor.
This book is full of life because of you.
—C.B.

Susie Mae sat by the window, sewing her best stitches. The glide of the needle through the fabric felt wonderful-good. She fancied her stitches to be the tiniest, the straightest anywhere.

My quilting is perfect, she decided.

Just like Mama's.

4

Aunt Martha broke the stillness. "Seems to me, Susie Mae looks more like her mama everyday."

Susie Mae looked up from her sewing and caught her mother's gaze. Mama *was* pretty, no doubt about it.

Susie Mae met up with big
brother Thomas. "Guess what
I overheard," she said, standing tall.
But Thomas paid her no mind.
"Aunt Martha says I look just like Mama!"
she boasted.

Thomas looked her over and scratched
his head. "Well, you may look like Mama,
but I doubt you can keep up with her all day."
Susie Mae straightened her apron.
"*Ach,* we'll just see about that…
starting tomorrow!"

"Cock-a-doodle do!" the rooster crowed at sunup.
Susie Mae chased Mama's skirt tail as they
hurried to the barn. "A good morning to yoodle-do!"
she called with glee.

Susie Mae scooted a tiny stool and the milk bucket smack-dab under Ol' Gerta. "I'm milking you today… like it or not."

A thin stream of milk *pink-pinged* against the sides of the pail. She glanced at Mama, thinking of cup cheese and sweet butter while Papa and Thomas pitched hay to the mules.

High in the rafters, a pigeon fluttered loudly. Susie Mae looked up, straining to see and…teetered off her milking stool.

Spritz-z-z! Warm milk squirted her face. It ran down her choring dress and apron, soaking her clean through.

"No…no!" she scolded the cow. But Ol' Gerta was not to blame. Stomping and mooing, the cow kicked over the bucket, spilling milk everywhere.

Susie Mae shouted, "This'll never do!"

Thomas frowned, and she stuck out her tongue at him.

"Aw, Susie Mae," said Mama softly, "Please, don't fret."

Susie Mae gathered eggs for breakfast. She peered
over her shoulder, wishing Thomas could see her now.
Such a fast worker she was!

"Keep your mind on your work,"
Mama prodded gently.

But as she dashed here and there,
Susie Mae dropped the eggs into
her basket too hard and…ach, no!
She broke one…two…three large eggs.
Hastily, she hid them, cracked and
oozing, under the straw. Mama would
never notice.

Berry picking with Mama was a delicious time.

Just this once, I'll gather more than I eat, thought Susie Mae. Quick as a wink, she placed each plump strawberry into her bucket.

Caw...caw. A crow swooped down and perched on the fence, giving Susie Mae a suspicious look.

"Don't worry, old bird," she whispered. "I can pick and not snitch."

Mama began to hum, moving swiftly between the rows. Joining in the song, Susie Mae picked the sun-ripened berries.

The singing and the sunshine made her stomach rumble. She could almost taste the juicy red strawberries with homemade ice cream.

One or two won't hurt, thought Susie Mae.

Old crow twitched his head, a spy in black.
"Never you mind," Susie Mae scolded, guarding
her secret.

Mama stopped picking to wipe her brow.
"How full is your bucket, dear one?"

Susie Mae looked at her bucket. "Just half,"
she confessed.

There was not a single stain on Mama's apron
or hands. "We'll gather more another day,"
Mama said without a frown.

"Time to wash up for lunch,"
Mama said, carrying her bucket, full to the brim.

Susie Mae hurried to catch up. "I'll set the table for you.
And I'll warm up the stew and clean up the kitchen, too."

"Why, *denki*—thank you, dear." Mama smiled ever so sweetly.

Matching her stride to Mama's, Susie Mae scurried past the barnyard,
toward the farmhouse.

Won't doubting Thomas be surprised? she thought, more than pleased
with herself.

Susie Mae stirred the beef stew while Mama
sliced tomatoes and cucumbers for the table.

When it was time, she reached for the ladle
to dish up. She was mindful of her older brother's eyes
on her, perhaps too much so. And accidentally,
she spilled some broth, scalding her finger. "Ouch!"

Mama rushed to her side. "Cold water will
help, dear."

Thomas was silent all the while.

Later, Susie Mae boasted again to Thomas.

"I've been mighty busy all day," she said.

"Seems to me, I'm just like Mama, after all!"

Thomas stopped pumping. "*Jah*, you can cook and clean, milk and pick berries, but…" He took off his hat, staring hard at it. "Aw, Susie Mae, there's a whole lot more to Mama than what she looks like and what she does."

"What do you mean?" she asked.

But in her heart, she knew.

Sure as sunshine, she did.

Susie Mae watched Mama reading the Good Book. *Dear Mama, ever patient and kind!* she thought.

Brushing tears away, she tiptoed near. "More than anything, Mama, I want to be just like you. Honest, I do."

Mama's smile was tender and warm. "I have a wonderful-good idea, dear one. Let's be more like the Lord Jesus…together."

"Jah, starting right now," Susie Mae whispered, hugging Mama ever so close.

31

In Lancaster County, church members attend "house church" at their neighbors' farm homes every other Lord's Day. The three-and-a-half-hour meeting takes place in large rooms where removable partitions make it possible to squeeze in up to one hundred twenty-five grown-ups and as many as one hundred fifty children.

There is lively fellowship outdoors upon first arriving, followed by silence as, one by one—beginning with the oldest members—the people enter the house of worship. Men and boys are seated together; women and young children sit in their own area. Unison a cappella singing soon begins, from the sixteenth-century hymnal called the *Ausbund*.

An opening sermon is given, then silent kneeling prayer, a Scripture by a deacon, and the main sermon. A second kneeling prayer is read aloud by the minister.

At the close of the meeting, a final blessing is prayed by the leader, the last hymn is sung, and there is a members' meeting. The women serve the noon meal, and after dessert, there is time for talking and visiting outdoors. From beginning to end, the day of worship represents the heart of Amish life: patience, unity, and humility.

"Off" Sundays are spent visiting family and friends, discussing Scripture, and reading Bible stories to the children.